Toot & Puddle

Wish You were Here

by Holly Hobbie

LITTLE, BROWN AND COMPANY
New York ⊰ Boston

Copyright © 2005 by Holly Hobbie and Douglas Hobbie

Little, Brown and Company

Time Warner Book Group
1271 Avenue of the Americas, New York, NY 10020
Visit our Web site at www.lb-kids.com

First Edition: September 2005

Library of Congress Cataloging-in-Publication Data
Hobbie, Holly.
  Toot & Puddle : Wish you were here / by Holly Hobbie.—1st ed.
    p. cm.
  Summary: Toot travels to Wildest Borneo for exotic plants, but when he
returns with the Violet Virus, it is up to Opal and Puddle to find a cure.
  ISBN 0-316-36602-1
  [1. Friendship—Fiction. 2. Plants—Fiction. 3. Travel—Fiction.
4. Pigs—Fiction.] I. Title: Toot and Puddle. II. Title: Wish you were here.
III. Title.
PZ7.H6517Toci 2005
[E]—dc22   2004009897

10 9 8 7 6 5 4 3 2 1

SC

Manufactured in China

The illustrations for this book were done in watercolor.
The text was set in Optima, and the display type was
hand-lettered by Holly Hobbie.

When Toot went off to Wildest Borneo, Opal came to Woodcock Pocket to keep her cousin, Puddle, company.

"What is Wildest Borneo, anyway?" she asked.

Puddle pointed to a green patch on Toot's globe. "It's a jungle," Puddle said, "boiling with heat and coiling with snakes and swarming with bugs."

"Why does Toot want to go there?"

"You know how Toot loves adventure, the wilder the better. And he has a passion for exotic plants. There are wildflowers in Wildest Borneo that you can't see anywhere else in the world."

"I would love to discover an exotic plant someday," Opal said.

Toot's first postcard arrived on the first day of May.

Dear Puds,
   Wildest Borneo is so lush and steamy. I've met the wildest pigs on earth, and I've found some of the wildest plants ever. You wouldn't believe the hairy indigo mud lily! And the giant wandering moon bloom gave me goose bumps.
   Hope Spring is bursting out in Woodcock Pocket.
                Your pal,
                Toot

To Puddle
Woodcock Pocket
U.S.A.

AIR MAIL

Puddle wanted his flower garden this year to be more dazzling than ever.

"Let's put the marigolds right next to the zinnias," he suggested.
"That will be perfect," Opal agreed. "How could the hairy
indigo mud lily be more beautiful than a marigold?"

Soon Puddle received another postcard—splattered with mud.

Dear Puds,
We finally discovered the imperial quaking Spice pod of Wildest Borneo.
Wish you were here!

Your buddy
Toot

To Puddle
WOODCOCK pocket
U.S.A

The next postcard didn't arrive for two weeks, when the lilacs
at Woodcock Pocket were beginning to bloom.

Dear Puds,
  A bit of bad luck. While exploring
Great Green Swamp, I was stung
by a fierce banded bush bee.
Ouch! The sting has given me
a case of the Violet virus, which
makes you pretty woozy.
  Don't worry, I'll be a lot
better once I get home
and get some rest.
          Your friend,
              Toot

To Puddle
Woodcock Pocket
U.S.A.

A week later Toot returned to Woodcock Pocket.

"Holy moly," Puddle gasped.
"I'm not myself these days," Toot admitted wearily.
"You're definitely . . . bluish," said Opal.
"Yes," Puddle agreed, "you're a pale shade of blue."
"I have the violet virus," Toot muttered. "That's the worst part. You turn blue."

"How soon will you be all better?" Opal asked.
"I don't know," Toot told her. "I've never had it before."

Opal and Puddle coddled Toot all day and into the night.
"Do you think you're feeling better?" she asked.
"I'm not sure," Toot answered.

In the morning Toot still felt qualmish and queasy and off-color.
"How do I look now?" he asked.
"I think you look a little better," Puddle ventured.
Outside the bedroom he asked Opal what she thought.
"I think he looks darker blue," she said. "I really do."
"I know," Puddle confessed.

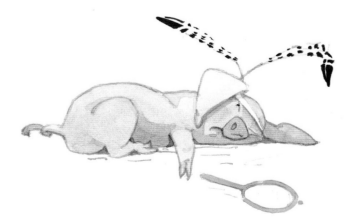

Puddle consulted the well-known healer, Dr. Willie. The doctor wasn't familiar with Toot's ailment, but he recommended quarts of green tea and jars of evening primrose oil.

"That's what Dr. Willie recommends for everything," Puddle told Opal.

Then he called Dr. Ha Song, hoping there might be a Chinese herbal remedy. Dr. Ha Song was aware of the violet virus, but he didn't believe there was a way to cure it. "A blue Toot is not so bad," he said.

The next day Puddle and Opal prepared a special PINK bath for Toot.
He soaked in the tub all morning, but the special bath didn't help.

Puddle had another idea. Maybe if they put their heads together and concentrated with all their might, they could wish Toot's violet virus away. They sat in a circle and held hands and tightly closed their eyes.

"Everyone think pink," Puddle whispered. "Let the violet virus be gone."

Opal was the first to open her eyes. "It's not working," she said.

Puddle was becoming discouraged. "I guess we could all get used to Toot's new color," he said.

"There must be someone who knows something about this problem," Opal insisted.

She stayed up late into the night learning about bees and hornets and stinging bugs on the World Wide Web. She read all she could about Wildest Borneo. Finally, in an obscure journal from England, she came upon an explorer who was an expert on the violet virus. He claimed that the only possible hope was a tea made from a mushroom called the purple slimecap stinkhorn.

"And guess what," said Opal. "The only place the purple slimecap stinkhorn is ever found is under very, very old bushes blooming with purple flowers."

Puddle knew of a large clump of lilacs that grew in a nearby meadow.

"They must be at least a hundred years old," he said.

"Go look!" cried Toot. "And good luck!"

Opal scrambled into the stand of ancient lilacs. Crawling into the dark tangle was like entering a cave. Lo and behold: shiny purplish stalks corkscrewed up from the damp, leafy ground.

"They stink!" Opal squealed excitedly. "They definitely stink!"

Back in Woodcock Pocket, Puddle simmered the smelly mushrooms in a large pot for three hours.

"Purple slimecap stinkhorn tea tastes awful," said Toot, crossing his eyes. "But I think I already feel better."

By morning Toot was his natural pinkish color again and he felt full of his usual vim and vigor. That evening he was ready to celebrate.

"Hooray for the purple slimecap stinkhorn," cheered Toot.

"And for the smart Englishman, too," Opal added.

"And especially for Opal," Puddle said proudly. "What would we have done without you?"

The next day, they decided, they would investigate the deep woods close to home. They had explored Woodcock Pocket many times, yet they never knew what they might discover.

Dear Brothers of Wildest Borneo
   I've completely recovered
from my bout of the violet
virus! And just the other
day we came upon a pink-
spotted star lily
right in Wildest
Woodcock Pocket.
Wish You were here!
   Cheers,
      TOOT

To
The Pigopig
General Delivery
Wildest Borneo